P9-BUI-799

THE NURSERY TREASURY

A Doubleday Book for Young Readers
PUBLISHED BY DELACORTE PRESS
a division of Bantam Doubleday Dell Publishing Group, Inc.
666 Fifth Avenue, New York, New York 10103

DOUBLEDAY
and the portrayal of an anchor with a dolphin
are trademarks of Bantam Doubleday Dell
Publishing Group, Inc.

Library of Congress Cataloging-in-Publication Data
The nursery treasury; a collection of baby games, rhymes
and lullabies / selected by Sally Emerson: illustrated by
Moira & Colin Maclean. — 1st ed. in U.S.A.
p.   cm.
Includes index.
Summary: Includes over 200 traditional rhymes, poems, lullabies,
and games with suggestions on how they may be used throughout
a child's day.
1. Nursery rhymes. 2. Children's poetry. 3. Lullabies.
(1. Nursery rhymes. 2. Lullabies. 3. Games.) I. Emerson, Sally,
1952-   II. Maclean, Moira, ill. III. Maclean, Colin, 1930-   ill,
PZ0.3.N938 1988
398'.8—dc19   88-12640   CIP   AC

ISBN 0-385-24650-1

This selection copyright © Sally Emerson 1988
Illustrations copyright © Kingfisher Books 1988
ALL RIGHTS RESERVED

PRINTED IN ITALY

10 9 8 7 6 5 4
GRI

THE NURSERY TREASURY

A COLLECTION OF BABY GAMES, RHYMES AND LULLABIES

SELECTED BY
SALLY EMERSON

ILLUSTRATED BY
MOIRA AND COLIN MACLEAN

A Doubleday Book for Young Readers

CONTENTS

BABY GAMES   10

A selection of playsongs for babies and toddlers.
There are tickle, touch, and rocking rhymes, knee
rides and bouncers as well as finger games and
simple action songs.

NURSERY SONGS   30

Favorite rhymes from traditional sources for you to
read and sing to your children.

DANCING & SINGING GAMES   54

Jumping, clapping, hopping, miming, and marching
songs as well as traditional children's games.

A WAS AN APPLE PIE   74

Delightful rhymes to introduce the letters of the
alphabet, numbers, days of the week, and months of
the year. There are memory rhymes and wise old
sayings, too.

STORY RHYMES   90

Well-loved nursery characters appear in fantastical,
funny, and familiar story rhymes.

LULLABIES   108

Enchanting poems and songs to lull children to sleep
—ideal for the end of the day.

INDEX OF FIRST LINES   122

BABY GAMES

11

1

Here sits Farmer Giles,
☆ *Touch his forehead.*

4
Here sits the hen,
☆ *Touch his lips.*

2

Here sit his two men,
☆ *Touch his eyes.*

5

Here sit the little chickens,
☆ *Touch his teeth.*

3

Here sits the
   cockadoodle,
☆ *Touch his nose.*

6

Here they run in,
Chin chopper,
Chin chopper,
Chin, chin, chin.
☆ *Tickle his chin.*

1

Knock at the door,
☆ *Tap her forehead.*

2

Ring the bell,
☆ *Tug her hair.*

3

Lift the latch,
☆ *Tweek her nose.*

4

And walk in.
☆ *Walk your fingers on her lips.*

Can you keep a secret?
I wonder if you can.
Don't laugh and don't cry
While it tickles in your hand.

☆ *Hands back to back, intertwine fingers.*

Here are the lady's
    knives and forks,

☆ *Turn hands over.*

Here's the lady's table,

☆ *Raise index fingers.*

Here's the lady's looking glass,

☆ *Raise little fingers and rock.*

And here's the baby's cradle.
Rock-rock, rock-rock, rock.

This little cow eats grass,
This little cow eats hay,
This little cow looks over the hedge,
This little cow runs away.
And this BIG cow does nothing at all
But lie in the fields all day!
We'll chase her.
    And chase her.
        And chase her!

☆ *A finger-counting rhyme, starting at the little finger. End by pouncing on the thumb.*

Dance, thumbkin, dance,
Dance, you merry men, every one;
But thumbkin, he can dance alone,
Thumbkin, he can dance.

☆ *Waggle thumb on its own, tucking the
four fingers into palm; then waggle all
fingers; then the thumb on its own again.
Repeat the game with each finger.*

Dance, Pointer, dance . . .
Dance, Longman, dance . . .
Dance, Ringman, dance . . .
Dance, Baby, dance . . .

1

Two little dicky birds,
Sitting on a wall,

2

One named Peter,
One named Paul.

3

Fly away, Peter!

4

Fly away, Paul!

5

Come back, Peter!
Come back, Paul!

Wee Wiggie,
Poke Piggie,
Tom Whistle,
John Gristle
And old BIG GOBBLE,
    gobble, gobble!

☆ *A toe-counting rhyme. Start with the little toe and end by seizing the big toe and pretending to gobble it up.*

This pig got into
the barn,
☆ *Start at the big toe.*

1

This ate all
the corn,

2

This said he
wasn't well,

3

This said he'd go
and tell,

4

And this said: "Squeak! squeak! squeak!
I can't get over the barn door sill."

5

This little pig went to market,
This little pig stayed at home,
This little pig had roast beef,
This little pig had none,
And this little pig cried:
"Wee-wee-wee-wee-wee-wee,"
All the way home!

☆ An old favorite – count from big to little toe
and end with a tickle.

Pat-a-cake, pat-a-cake, baker's man,
Bake me a cake as fast as you can;
Pat it and prick it and mark it with B,
Put it in the oven for baby and me.

☆ *A hand-patting rhyme for babies and a first clapping song for toddlers. Act out the rhyme by pretending to prick the baby's palm and tracing a B on it.*

Handy Pandy,
Sugar Candy,
Which one will you choose,
Top or bottom?

☆ *Hide something in one hand. Then put one closed fist over the other. The game is to choose the right hand.*

18

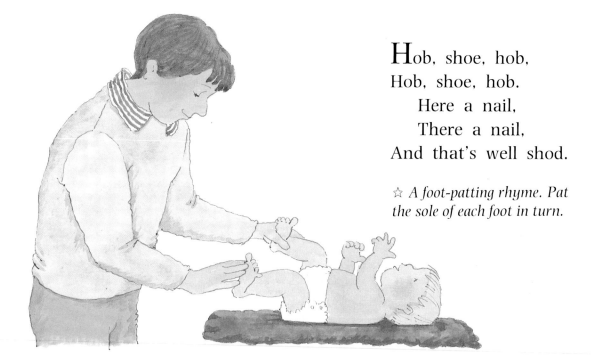

Hob, shoe, hob,
Hob, shoe, hob.
    Here a nail,
    There a nail,
And that's well shod.

☆ *A foot-patting rhyme. Pat*
the sole of each foot in turn.

Leg over leg,
As the dog goes to Dover,
When he comes to a wall,
Jump! He goes over!

☆ *Sit the baby in your lap with his back*
to you. Cross and uncross his legs in time
to the first three lines. At JUMP lift both
legs up so that he topples back into you.

1

F̲ather and Mother and Uncle John
Went to market, one by one.
☆ *Jog the baby gently.*

2

Father fell off!
☆ *Drop her to one side.*

3

Mother fell off!
☆ *Drop her to the other side.*

4

But Uncle John went on, and on,
And on, and on and on.
☆ *Now bounce faster and faster.*

This is the way the ladies ride,
Nimble-nim, nimble-nim;

This is the way the gentlemen ride,
Gallop-a-trot! Gallop-a-trot!

This is the way the farmers ride,
Jiggety-jog, jiggety-jog;

This is the way the butcher boy rides,
Tripperty-trot, tripperty-trot,

Till he falls in a ditch with a flipperty,
Flipperty, flop, flop, FLOP!

☆ *This knee ride gets faster and faster. End
with a sudden drop between your knees.*

21

Jelly on the plate,
Jelly on the plate,
Wibble wobble,
Wibble wobble,
Jelly on the plate.

☆ *Wobble from side to side.*

Biscuits in the tin,
Biscuits in the tin,
Shake them up,
Shake them up,
Biscuits in the tin.

☆ *Shake up and down.*

Fire on the floor,
Fire on the floor,
Stamp it out,
Stamp it out,
Fire on the floor.

☆ *Bounce to the ground and up.*

Candles on the cake,
Candles on the cake,
Blow them out,
Blow them out,
Puff puff puff.

☆ *Blow each other gently.*

☆ A bouncing rhyme.

Dance to your daddy,
  My little baby,
Dance to your daddy,
  My little lamb.

You shall have a fishy,
  In a little dishy,
You shall have a fishy,
  When the boat comes in.

Rigadoon, rigadoon,
Now let him fly,
Sit him on father's foot,
Jump him up high.

☆ *Cross your legs and sit the*
baby on your crossed ankle.
Swing up and down.

☆ *Toddlers will enjoy acting out this rhyme.*

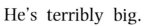

The elephant goes like this, like that,

He's terribly big.

And he's terribly fat.

He has no fingers,

He has no toes,

But goodness, gracious, what a nose!

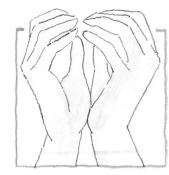   

Here is a ball for baby, Big and soft and round.

Here is a baby's hammer, See how it can pound.

Here is a baby's trumpet, Tootle tootle toot.

Here is the way my baby Plays peek-a-boo Boo!

☆ *A favorite tickling rhyme.*

Round and round the garden
Like a teddy bear.
One step, two step,
Tickle you under there!

25

Ring-a-ring o'roses,
A pocket full of posies,
A-tishoo! A-tishoo!
We all fall down.

☆ Choose either of the two second verses to start again. Older children will love the race in the second version.

The cows are in the meadow,
Eating buttercups,
A-tishoo! A-tishoo!
We all get up.

The cows are in the meadow,
Eating all the grass,
A-tishoo! A-tishoo!
Who's up last?
NOT ME!

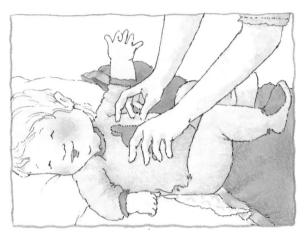

What shall we do with
  a lazy Katie?
What shall we do with
  a lazy Katie?
What shall we do with
  a lazy Katie?
Early in the morning.

Roll her on the bed and
  tickle her all over,
Roll her on the bed and
  tickle her all over,
Roll her on the bed and
  tickle her all over,
Early in the morning.

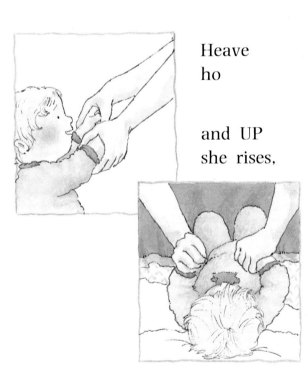

Heave
ho

and UP
she rises,

Heave ho and UP she rises,
Heave ho and UP she rises,
Early in the morning.

♫ *Sing to the tune of "What shall we
do with the drunken sailor?"*

Jack-in-the-box jumps UP
  like this,
☆ *Swing him up high.*

He makes me laugh when he
  waggles his head,
☆ *Shake him gently.*

I gently press him
  down again,
☆ *Lower him down.*

But Jack-in-the-box
  jumps UP instead.
☆ *Swing him up again.*

Ride a cockhorse to Banbury Cross,
To see a fine lady upon a white horse;
Rings on her fingers,
And bells on her toes,
She shall have music
wherever she goes.

☆ *A rhyme for knee rides.*

Rock, rock, rock your boat,
Gently down the stream,
Merrily, merrily, merrily, merrily,
Life is but a dream.

☆ *Rock small babies from side to side.*
Pull older ones up to sitting position and
back again.

A trot, a canter,
A gallop and over,
Out of the saddle
And roll in the clover.

☆ *One last knee ride. End by swinging*
the baby right out of the ''saddle'' down
to the ground.

NURSERY SONGS

Humpty Dumpty sat on a wall,
Humpty Dumpty had a great fall;
All the King's horses,
And all the King's men,
Couldn't put Humpty together again.

Old King Cole was a merry old soul,
And a merry old soul was he;
    He called for his pipe,
    And he called for his bowl,
And he called for his fiddlers three.

Every fiddler, he had a fiddle,
And a very fine fiddle had he;
    Oh, there's none so rare
    As can compare
With King Cole and his fiddlers three.

I had a little nut tree,
    Nothing would it bear
But a silver nutmeg
    And a golden pear;
The king of Spain's daughter
    Came to visit me,
And all for the sake
    Of my little nut tree.

Little Boy Blue,
Come blow your horn.
The sheep's in the meadow,
The cow's in the corn.
Where is the boy
Who looks after the sheep?
He's under a haystack
Fast asleep.
Will you wake him?
No, not I,
For if I do,
He's sure to cry.

Ladybird, ladybird,
Fly away home,
Your house is on fire
Your children all gone;
All but one,
And her name is Ann,
And she has crept under
The warming pan.

Lavender's blue, dilly, dilly,
    Lavender's green;
When I am king, dilly, dilly,
    You shall be queen.

Call up your men, dilly, dilly,
    Set them to work,
Some to the plow, dilly, dilly,
    Some to the cart.

Some to make hay, dilly, dilly,
    Some to thresh corn,
Whilst you and I, dilly, dilly,
    Keep ourselves warm.

Old Macdonald had a farm,
Eee, aye, eee, aye, oh.
And on that farm he had some cows,
Eee, aye, eee, aye, oh.
With a moo-moo here,
And a moo-moo there,
Here a moo, there a moo,
Everywhere a moo-moo,
Old Macdonald had a farm,
Eee, aye, eee, aye, oh.

Old Macdonald had a farm,
Eee, aye, eee, aye, oh.
And on that farm he had some . . .
pigs . . . sheep . . . horses . . .
cats . . . dogs . . . ducks.

☆ *Repeat the song with different animals and noises.*

Three blind mice! Three blind mice!
See how they run! See how they run!
They all ran after the farmer's wife,
Who cut off their tails with a carving knife;
Did you ever see such a thing in your life,
     As three blind mice?

Hickory, dickory, dock,
The mouse ran up the clock.
     The clock struck one,
     The mouse ran down,
Hickory, dickory, dock.

Ding, dong, bell,
Pussy's in the well.
Who put her in?
    Little Johnny Green.
Who pulled her out?
    Little Tommy Stout.
What a naughty boy was that
To try to drown poor pussycat,
Who never did him any harm,
But killed the mice in his father's barn.

I love little pussy,
    Her coat is so warm,
And if I don't hurt her
    She'll do me no harm.

So I'll not pull her tail,
    Nor drive her away,
But pussy and I
    Very gently will play.

She shall sit by my side,
    And I'll give her some food;
And pussy will love me
    Because I am good.

There was a little girl,
And she had a little curl
Right in the middle of her forehead;
When she was good,
She was very, very good,
But when she was bad,
She was horrid.

Tom, Tom, the piper's son,
Stole a pig and away he run;
The pig was eat,
And Tom was beat,
And Tom went howling
Down the street.

Georgie Porgie, pudding and pie,
Kissed the girls and made them cry.
When the boys came out to play,
Georgie Porgie ran away.

It's raining, it's pouring,
The old man's snoring;
He got into bed
And bumped his head
And couldn't get up in
    the morning.

Doctor Foster went to Gloucester
In a shower of rain;
    He stepped in a puddle,
    Right up to his middle,
And never went there again.

One misty, moisty morning,
    When cloudy was the weather,
I met a little old man
    Clothed all in leather.

He began to compliment,
    And I began to grin,
How do you do, and how do you do,
    And how do you do again?

40

Rain, rain, go away,
Come again another day,
All the children want to play.
Rain, rain, go to Spain,
Never show your face again.

Rub-a-dub-dub,
    Three men in a tub,
And who do you think they be?
    The butcher, the baker,
    The candlestick maker;
Turn 'em out, knaves all three!

Sing a song of sixpence,
    A pocket full of rye;
Four-and-twenty blackbirds,
    Baked in a pie.

When the pie was opened,
    The birds began to sing;
Was not that a dainty dish,
    To set before the king?

The king was in his counting house,
    Counting out his money;
The queen was in the parlor,
    Eating bread and honey.

The maid was in the garden,
    Hanging out the clothes,
When down came a blackbird
    And pecked off her nose.

☆ *Happy ending:*
Along came Jenny Wren
And stuck her nose back on again.

Oh, do you know the muffin man,
The muffin man, the muffin man?
Oh, do you know the muffin man
Who lives in Drury Lane?

Polly, put the kettle on,
Polly, put the kettle on,
Polly, put the kettle on,
　　We'll all have tea.

Sukey, take it off again,
Sukey, take it off again,
Sukey, take it off again,
　　They've all gone away.

Hot cross buns! Hot cross buns!
One a penny, two a penny,
　　hot cross buns.
If you have no daughters,
Give them to your sons.
One a penny, two a penny,
　　hot cross buns.

44

Pease porridge hot,
Pease porridge cold,
Pease porridge in the pot,
Nine days old.

Some like it hot,
Some like it cold,
Some like it in the pot,
Nine days old.

Jack Sprat could eat no fat,
His wife could eat no lean,
And so between them both, you see,
They licked the platter clean.

Baa, baa, black sheep,
   Have you any wool?
Yes, sir, yes, sir,
   Three bags full;

One for the master,
   And one for the dame,
Ane one for the little boy
   Who lives down the lane.

Mary, Mary, quite contrary,
   How does your garden grow?
With silver bells and cockle shells,
   And pretty maids all in a row.

Christmas is coming,
    The geese are getting fat,
Please to put a penny
    In the old man's hat.
If you haven't got a penny,
    A ha'penny will do;
If you haven't got a ha'penny,
    Then God bless you!

Little Jack Horner
Sat in the corner,
Eating his Christmas pie;
    He put in his thumb,
    And pulled out a plum,
And said: "What a good boy am I!"

Jingle, bells! Jingle, bells!
    Jingle all the way;
Oh, what fun it is to ride
    In a one-horse open sleigh.

Goosey, goosey gander,
  Whither shall I wander?
Upstairs and downstairs
  And in my lady's chamber.
There I met an old man
  Who would not say his prayers,
I took him by the left leg
  And threw him down the stairs.

Hickety, pickety, my black hen,
She lays eggs for gentlemen;
Sometimes one, and sometimes ten,
Hickety, pickety, my black hen.

Up and down the City Road,
    In and out the Eagle,
That's the way the money goes,
    Pop goes the weasel!

Half a pound of tuppeny rice,
    Half a pound of treacle,
Mix it up and make it nice,
    Pop goes the weasel!

Ipsey Wipsey spider,
    Climbing up the spout;
Down came the rain
    And washed the spider out.

Out came the sunshine
    And dried up all the rain;
Ipsey Wipsey spider,
    Climbing up again.

Yankee Doodle came to town,
  Riding on a pony;
He stuck a feather in his cap
  and called it macaroni.

First he bought a porridge pot,
  And then he bought a ladle,
And then he trotted home again
  As fast as he was able.

Bobby Shaftoe's gone to sea,
Silver buckles on his knee;
He'll come back and marry me,
  Bonny Bobby Shaftoe.

Bobby Shaftoe's bright and fair,
Combing down his yellow hair;
He's my love for evermore,
  Bonny Bobby Shaftoe.

O dear, what can the matter be?
Dear, dear, what can the matter be?
O dear, what can the matter be?
  Johnny's so long at the fair.

He promised he'd buy me a fairing should please me,
And then for a kiss, oh! he vowed he would tease me,
He promised he'd bring me a bunch of blue ribbons
  To tie up my bonny brown hair.

And it's O dear, what can the matter be?
Dear, dear, what can the matter be?
O dear, what can the matter be?
  Johnny's so long at the fair.

Peter, Peter, pumpkin eater,
  Had a wife and couldn't keep her;
He put her in a pumpkin shell,
  And there he kept her very well.

Hey diddle, diddle,
The cat and the fiddle,
The cow jumped over the moon;
The little dog laughed
To see such sport,
And the dish ran away with the spoon.

Girls and boys, come out to play,
The moon doth shine as bright as day.
Leave your supper and leave your sleep,
And come with your playfellows into the street.
Come with a whoop and come with a call,
Come with a good will or not at all.
Up the ladder and down the wall,
A half-penny loaf will serve us all;
You find milk, and I'll find flour,
And we'll have a pudding in half an hour.

54

DANCING & SINGING GAMES

Head and shoulders, knees and toes,
    knees and toes,
Head and shoulders, knees and toes,
    knees and toes,

☆ *Touch each part of the*
body as you sing.

And eyes, and ears, and mouth and nose,
Head and shoulders, knees and toes,
    knees and toes.

If you're happy and you know it,
    clap your hands,
If you're happy and you know it,
    clap you're hands,
If you're happy and you know it,
    and you really want to show it,
If you're happy and you know it,
    clap your hands.

If you're happy and you know it,
    stamp your feet . . .
If you're happy and you know it,
    nod your head . . .
If you're happy and you know it,
    shout "Hooray!" . . .

☆ *Copy the actions.*

Teddybear, teddybear,
dance on your toes.

Teddybear, teddybear,
touch your nose.

Teddybear, teddybear,
stand on your head.

Teddybear, teddybear,
go to bed.

Teddybear, teddybear,
wake up now.

Teddybear, teddybear,
make your bow.

Teddybear, teddybear,
touch the ground.

Teddybear, teddybear,
turn right around.

Teddybear, teddybear,
run upstairs.

Teddybear, teddybear,
say your prayers.

Teddybear, teddybear,
turn off the light.

Teddybear, teddybear,
say goodnight.

Oh, the grand old Duke of York,
He had ten thousand men.
   He marched them up
   to the top of the hill
And he marched them down again.

And when they were up they were up,
And when they were down they were down,
And when they were only halfway up
They were neither up nor down.

☆ *Sit the baby or toddler in your lap and walk his
legs or jog in time to the song. Swing him UP and
DOWN at those words. Older children will enjoy
marching in time, jumping UP and crouching
DOWN, and acting out the additional verses below.
Repeat the second chorus after each new verse.*

Oh, the grand old Duke of York,
He had ten thousand men.
   They beat their drums
   to the top of the hill
And they beat them down again.

They played their pipes to the top of the hill . . .
They banged their guns to the top of the hill . . .

Can you walk on tiptoe
As softly as a cat?

Can you stamp along the road
STAMP, STAMP, just like that?

Can you take some great big strides
Just like a giant can?

Or walk along so slowly,
Like a bent old man?

Stepping over stepping-stones,
   One, two, three,
Stepping over stepping-stones,
   Come with me.
   The river's very fast,
   And the river's very wide,
And we'll step across on stepping-stones
   And reach the other side.

Jack, be nimble,
Jack, be quick,
Jack, JUMP over
    the candlestick.

*☆ With a baby, try crossing your legs
and sitting him on the top ankle facing
you. Hold his hands and swing him up
and down. At JUMP swing him into the
air and onto your knee.*

Here am I,
    Little Jumping Joan;
When nobody's with me
    I'm all alone.

Handy Pandy, Jack-a-dandy,
Loves plum cake and sugar candy,
He bought some at the grocer's shop,
And out he came, hop, hop, hop!

American jump! American jump!
One—Two—Three!
Under the water catching fishes,
Catching fishes for my tea.
      Dead . . .
      Or alive . . .
      Or around the world?

☆ *Holding the child under her arms or by the hands, jump her up three times. Catch her around her waist at THREE, then lower her backward to catch a fish, and offer a choice of "Dead or alive or around the world."*
For DEAD, lower her to the ground.
For ALIVE, swing her up high.
For AROUND THE WORLD, swing her over your back and down again.

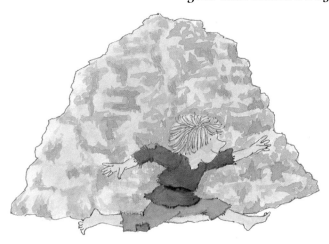

Round and round the rugged rock
The ragged rascal ran.
How many R's are there in that?
Now tell me if you can.

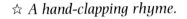

☆ A hand-clapping rhyme.

Miss Polly had a dolly
   who was sick, sick, sick,
So she phoned for the doctor
   to be quick, quick, quick.
The doctor came
   with her bag and her hat,
And she knocked on the door
   with a rat-a-tat-tat.

She looked at the dolly
   and she shook her head,
And she said, "Miss Polly,
   put her straight to bed."
She wrote on a paper
   for a pill, pill, pill.
"I'll be back in the morning
   with my bill, bill, bill."

One day I went to sea,
   chop, knee,
To see what I could see,
   chop, knee,
But all that I could see,
   chop, knee,
Was the bottom of the
   deep blue sea,
   chop, knee.

☆ This clapping song gets faster and faster.
Clap each other's hands until SEA, clap your
own hands at CHOP, and pat your knees at KNEE.

Oh, we can play on the big bass drum,
    And this is the way we do it:
"BOOM, BOOM, BOOM" goes the big bass drum,
    And that's the way we do it.

Oh, we can play on the little flute,
    And this is the way we do it:
"TOOTLE TOOTLE TOOT" goes the little flute,
    And that's the way we do it.

Oh, we can play on the tambourine,
    And this is the way we do it:
"TING, TING, TING" goes the tambourine,
    And that's the way we do it.

☆ *The song continues changing the instrument
each time. Older children may like to
add the noise of the new instrument with
each verse until you have the whole band.*

"FIDDLE-DIDDLE-DEE" goes the violin . . .
"TICKA TICKA TECK" go the castanets . . .
"ZOOM, ZOOM, ZOOM" goes the double bass . . .
"TA TA TARA" goes the bugle horn . . .

63

See-saw, Margery Daw,
Johnny shall have a new master;
He shall have but a penny a day,
Because he can't work any faster.

Sally go round the sun,
Sally go round the moon,
Sally go round the chimney-pots
On a Saturday afternoon.

☆ *A good swinging rhyme. Also a favorite for ring dancing.*

Swing me low
Swing me high,
Over the grasses
As high as the sky.
Hair flying out.
Wind rushing by,
Like birds in the blue,
We sing as we fly,
Higher . . .
Fly . . .

☆ *Skipping rhymes.*

What's your name?
Johnny Maclean.
Where do you live?
Down the lane.
What's your shop?
Lollypop.
What's your number?
Cucumber.

What's your name?
Mary Jane.
Where do you live?
Cabbage Lane.
What's your number?
Rain and thunder.
What address?
Watercress.

The wood was dark
The grass was green,
Up comes Sally
With a tambourine.
Alpaca frock,
New scarf shawl,
White straw bonnet
And a pink parasol.

I went to the river
No ship to get across,
I paid ten shillings
For an old blind horse.
I up on his back
And off in a crack,
Sally, tell my mother
I shall never come back.

Oranges and lemons,
Say the bells of St. Clements.

I owe you five farthings,
Say the bells of St. Martins.

When will you pay me?
Say the bells of Old Bailey.

When I grow rich,
Say the bells at Shoreditch.

When will that be?
Say the bells of Stepney.

I'm sure I don't know,
Says the great bell at Bow.

Here-comes-a-candle-to-light-you-to-bed,
Here-comes-a-chopper-to-chop-off-your-head,
Chip-chop-chip-chop the-last-man's . . . HEAD

London Bridge is falling down, Build it up with iron bars,
Falling down, falling down, Iron bars, iron bars,
London Bridge is falling down, Build it up with iron bars,
    My fair lady. My fair lady.

Here's a prisoner I have got,
I have got, I have got,
Here's a prisoner I have got,
    My fair lady.

☆ You need at least six six children for these two games. Choose London Bridge for younger or more shy children.

Two children form an arch (or two adults if the children are too short!); the others skip in a circle passing under the arch until the last lines.

For Oranges and Lemons the arch then pretends to chop the children as they pass through at CHIP and CHOP and captures one in their arms at HEAD.

The two sides of the arch are the Oranges and the Lemons, and the captive is asked to choose which he wants to be. This is done in secret so that the others don't know which side is which.

For London Bridge, a child is trapped at HERE'S A PRISONER and chooses to stand behind one of the people forming the arch.

The game is repeated until everyone has been caught. Then the two teams behind each side of the arch have a tug of war.

I'm a little teapot,
Short and stout,
Here's my handle,
Here's my spout.
When I see the teacups,
Hear me shout:
"Tip me up and pour me out!"

☆ *Do the actions as you sing.*

I can tie my shoelaces,
I can brush my hair,
I can wash my face and hands
And dry myself with care.

I can clean my teeth, too,
And fasten up my frocks,
I can dress all by myself
And pull up both my socks.

Here we go round the mulberry bush,
The mulberry bush, the mulberry bush,
Here we go round the mulberry bush,
On a cold and frosty morning.

☆ Join hands and dance in a circle. Stop to do
the actions of the next verses, repeating the
first verse and its dance after each one.

This is the way we wash our hands,
Wash our hands, wash our hands;
This is the way we wash our hands,
On a cold and frosty morning.

This is the way we wash our face . . .
This is the way we brush our hair . . .
This is the way we clean our teeth . . .
This is way we put on our clothes . . .

The Farmer's in the den,
The Farmer's in the den,
Eee-Aye-Eee-Aye,
The Farmer's in the den.

The Farmer wants a Wife . . .
The Wife wants a Child . . .
The Child wants a Nurse . . .
The Nurse wants a Dog . . .
The Dog wants a Bone . . .

We all pat the Bone,
We all pat the Bone,
Eee-Aye-Eee-Aye,
We all pat the Bone.

☆ *A game for at least six children. One child is chosen to be the farmer and the others join hands and dance around him as they sing. They stop for the farmer to choose a wife, who joins him inside the ring. The circle dances around again for the next verse, and so on until everybody pats the bone.*

The wheels on the bus go round and round
Round and round, round and round.
The wheels on the bus go round and round,
All day long.
☆ *Rotate arms like wheels.*

The wipers on the bus go swish, swish, swish . . .
☆ *Wave hands from side to side.*

The driver on the bus goes: "Toot, toot, toot" . . .
☆ *Press imaginary horn with thumb.*

The people on the bus go: "Yakkity-yak!" . . .
☆ *Open and shut fingers.*

The children on the bus make too much NOISE . . .
☆ *Hands over ears, shout NOISE.*

The babies on the bus fall fast asleep . . .
☆ *Head on hands as if asleep and whisper lines.*

Here we go looby-loo,
Here we go looby-light,
Here we go looby-loo,
All on a Saturday night.

Put your right hand in,
Put your right hand out,
Shake it a little, a little,
And turn yourself about.

Put your left hand in . . .
Put your right foot in . . .
Put your left foot in . . .
Put your whole self in . . .

☆ *Join hands and dance in a circle.*
Stop to do the actions of the second
verse, and so on, repeating the first
verse and dance after each new verse.

Three times around went our gallant, gallant ship,
And three times around went she;
Three times around went our gallant, gallant ship,
Till she sank to the bottom of the sea.

*☆ Join hands and dance in a circle.
Everybody falls down at the last line.*

"Pull her up, pull her up," said the little sailor boy,
   "Pull her up, pull her up," said he,
"Pull her up, pull her up," said the little sailor boy,
   "Or she'll sink to the bottom of the sea."

☆ Still holdings hands, pull each other up again.

I sent a letter to my love
And on the way I dropped it,
A little puppy picked it up
And put it in his pocket.
It isn't you, it isn't you,
   But it is you.

☆ The children stand or sit in a circle. One child has been chosen to be "it" and walks around the circle. On "it is you" he drops the letter (any small object) behind a child. That child picks it up and races around in the opposite direction to get back to his place before the first child reaches it. Whoever is left out becomes "it."

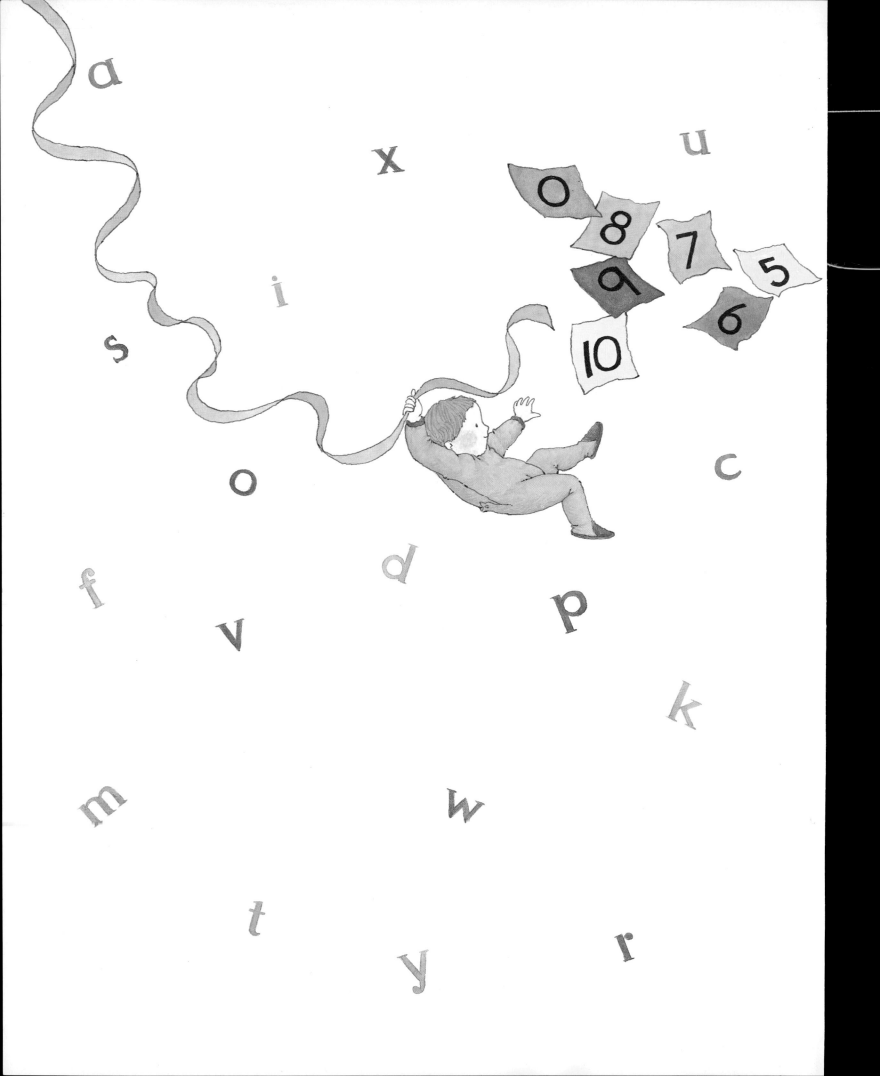

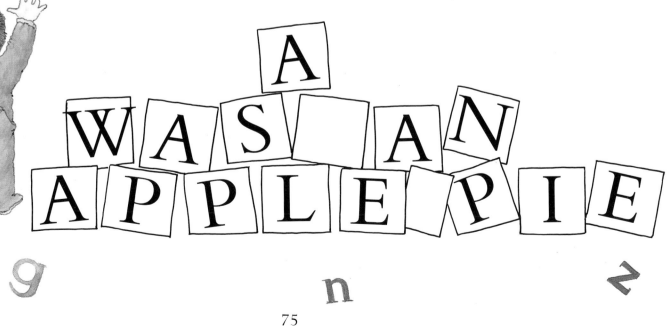

A

A was an apple pie

B

B bit it

C

C cut it

D

D dealt it

E

E eat it

F

F fought for it

G

G got it

H

H had it

I

I inspected it

J

J jumped for it

K

K kept it

L

L longed for it

M

M mourned for it

N

N nodded at it

O

O opened it

P

P peeped in it

Q

Q quartered it

R

R ran for it

S

S sang for it

T

T took it

U

U upset it

V

V viewed it

W

W wanted it

XYZ

XYZ and & all wished
for a piece in hand.

There were five in the bed and
the little one said: "Roll over! Roll over!"
So they all rolled over and one fell out.

There were four in the bed . . .
There were three in the bed . . .
There were two in the bed . . .

There was one in the bed,
And that little one said:
"Good, now I've got the bed to
myself, I'm going to stretch
and stretch and stretch!"

☆ *Both of these rhymes can be played
with five children or toys.*

Five brown teddies sitting on a wall,
Five brown teddies sitting on a wall,
And if one brown teddy should accidentally fall,
They'd be four brown teddies sitting on a wall.

♫ *Sing to a the tune of
"Ten Green Bottles."*

Four brown teddies sitting on a wall . . .
Three brown teddies sitting on a wall . . .
Two brown teddies sitting on a wall . . .
One brown teddy sitting on a wall,
One brown teddy sitting on a wall,
And if one brown teddy should accidentally fall,
There'd be no brown teddies sitting there at all!

One two, three, four, five,
    Once I caught a fish alive,
Six, seven, eight, nine, ten,
    Then I threw it back again.
Why did you let it go?
    Because it bit my finger so.
Which finger did it bite?
    This little finger on the right.

1 2, 3, 4,
    Mary at the kitchen door,
5, 6, 7, 8,
    Counting cherries off a plate.

Tinker,   Lady,
Tailor,   Baby,
Soldier,   Gipsy
Sailor,   Queen.
Richman,   This year,
Poorman,   Next year,
Beggerman,   Sometime,
Thief.   Never.

79

One, two,
Buckle my shoe;

Three, four,
Knock at the door;

Five, six,
Pick up sticks;

Seven, eight,
Lay them straight;

Nine, ten,
A big fat hen;

Eleven, twelve,
Dig and delve;

Thirteen, fourteen,
Maids a-courting;

Fifteen, sixteen,
Maids in the kitchen;

Seventeen, eighteen,
Maids in waiting;

Nineteen, twenty,
My plate's empty.

The cock does crow
To let you know
If you be wise
'Tis time to rise;
For early to bed
And early to rise,
Is the way to be healthy
And wealthy and wise.

See a pin and pick it up,
　　All the day you'll have good luck.
See a pin and let it lay,
　　Bad luck you'll have all the day.

Mackerel sky,
Mackerel sky,
Not long wet
And not long dry.

82

Manners in the dining room,
Manners in the hall,
If you don't behave yourself,
You shan't have none at all.

A wise old owl sat in an oak,
The more he heard the less he spoke;
The less he spoke the more he heard.
Why aren't we all like that wise old bird?

Red sky at night,
Shepherd's delight;
Red sky in the morning,
Shepherd's warning.

Go to bed late,
Stay very small;
Go to bed early,
Grow very tall.

Monday's child
is fair of face,

Tuesday's child
is full of grace,

Wednesday's child
is full of woe,

Thursday's child
has far to go,

Friday's child
is loving and giving,

Saturday's child
works hard for its living,

And the child that's born on the Sabbath day
Is bonny and blithe, and good and gay.

Thirty days hath September,
April, June, and November;
All the rest have thirty-one,
Excepting February alone;
And that has twenty-eight days clear
And twenty-nine in each leap year.

Mr. East gave a feast;
Mr. North laid the cloth;
Mr. West did his best;
Mr. South burned his mouth
With eating a cold potato.

Cuckoo, cuckoo, what do you do?
In April I open my bill;
In May I sing all day;
In June I change my tune;
In July away I fly;
In August away I must.

Tom Thumb's Picture Alphabet

A was an archer and shot at a frog;

B was a butcher and had a great dog.

C was a captain, all covered with lace;

D was a drummer and had a red face.

E was an esquire with pride on his brow;

F was a farmer and followed the plow.

G was a gamester who had but ill-luck;

H was a hunter and hunted a buck.

I was an innkeeper who loved to carouse;

J was a joiner and built up a house.

K was a king, so mighty and grand;

L was a lady and had a white hand.

M was a miser and hoarded up gold;

N was a
nobleman,
gallant
and bold.

O was an oyster
girl and went
about town;

P was a parson
and wore a
black gown.

Q was a queen
who wore a
silk slip;

R was robber
and wanted
a whip.

S was a sailor
and spent all
he got;

T was a tinker
and mended
a pot.

U was a userer,
a miserable
elf;

V was a vintner
who drank all
himself.

W was a watchman
and guarded
the door;

X was expensive
and so became
poor.

Y was a youth
and did not
love school;

Z was a zany,
a poor
harmless fool.

Five little monkeys walked
along the shore,

One went a'sailing,

Then there were four.

Four little monkeys
climbed up a tree,
One tumbled down,

Then there were three.

Three little monkeys found
a pot of glue,

One got stuck in it,

Then there were two.

Two little monkeys found
a currant bun,

One ran away with it,

Then there was one,

One little monkey
and his little wife,
Lived in a banana tree
for the rest of his life.

"Bow-wow," says the dog,
"Mew, mew," says the cat,
"Grunt, grunt," goes the hog,
And "Squeak" goes the rat.
"Tu-whu," says the owl,
"Caw, caw," says the crow,
"Quack, quack," says the duck,
And what cuckoos say you know.

cuckoo!

One for sorrow, two for joy,
Three for a girl, four for a boy,
Five for silver, six for gold,
Seven for a secret ne'er to be told.

I'll tell you a story
About Jack-a-Nory,
    And now my story's begun;
I'll tell you another
About Jack and his brother,
    And now my story is done.

STORY RHYMES

Mary had a little lamb,
    Its fleece was white as snow;
And everywhere that Mary went
    The lamb was sure to go.

It followed her to school one day,
    That was against the rule;
It made the children laugh and play
    To see a lamb at school.

And so the teacher turned it out,
    But still it lingered near,
And waited patiently about
    Till Mary did appear.

"Why does the lamb love Mary so?"
    The eager children cry;
"Why, Mary loves the lamb, you know,"
    The teacher did reply.

Jack and Jill
Went up the hill,
To fetch a pail of water;
Jack fell down,
And broke his crown,
And Jill came tumbling after.

Then up Jack got,
And home did trot,
As fast as he could caper;
To old Dame Dob,
Who patched his nob
With vinegar and brown paper.

Three little kittens
They lost their mittens,
And they began to cry,
"Oh, Mother dear, we sadly fear
Our mittens we have lost."

"What! lost your mittens,
You naughty kittens!
Then you shall have no pie.
Mee-ow, mee-ow, mee-ow.
No, you shall have no pie."

The three little kittens
They found their mittens,
And they began to cry,
"Oh, Mother dear,
see here, see here,
Our mittens we have found."

"Put on your mittens,
You silly kittens,
And you shall have some pie."
"Purr-r, purr-r, purr-r,
Oh, let us have some pie."

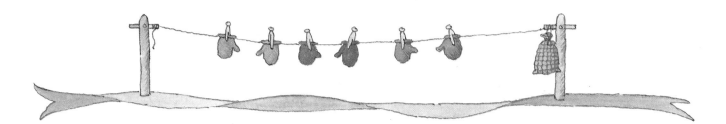

The three little kittens
Put on their mittens
And soon ate up the pie;
"Oh, Mother dear, we greatly fear
Our mittens we have soiled."

"What! soiled your mittens,
You naughty kittens!"
Then they began to sigh,
    "Mee-ow, mee-ow, mee-ow,"
Then they began to sigh.

The three little kittens
They washed their mittens,
And hung them out to dry;
"Oh mother dear, do you not hear?
Our mittens we have washed."

"What! washed your mittens,
You good little kittens,
But I smell a rat close by."
    "Mee-ow, mee-ow, mee-ow,
We smell a rat close by."

Little Piggy

Where are you going, you little pig?
I'm leaving my mother, I'm growing so big!
   So big, young pig!
   So young, so big!
What, leaving your mother,
   you foolish young pig?

   Where are you going, you little pig?
   I've got a new spade, and I'm going to dig!
     To dig, little pig!
     A little pig dig!
   Well, I never saw a pig with a spade
     that could dig!

Where are you going, you little pig?
Why, I'm going to have a nice ride in a gig!
   In a gig, little pig!
   What, a pig in a gig!
Well, I never yet saw a pig in a gig!

Where are you going, you little pig?
I'm going to the barber's to buy me a wig!
    A wig, little pig!
    A pig in a wig!
Why, whoever before saw a pig in a wig!

Where arc you going, you little pig?
Why, I'm going to the ball to dance a fine jig!
    A jig, little pig!
    A pig dance a jig!
Well, I never before saw a pig dance a jig!

THOMAS HOOD

The Queen of Hearts
She made some tarts,
All on a summer's day;
The Knave of Hearts
He stole the tarts,
And took them clean away.

The King of Hearts
Called for the tarts,
And beat the knave full sore;
The Knave of Hearts
Brought back the tarts,
And vowed he'd steal no more.

Pussycat, pussycat,
    Where have you been?
I've been to London
    To look at the Queen.

Pussycat, pussycat,
    What did you there?
I frightened a little mouse
    Under her chair.

99

The Owl and the Pussycat

The Owl and the Pussycat went to sea
    In a beautiful pea-green boat:
They took some honey, and plenty of money
    Wrapped up in a five-pound note.

The Owl looked up to the stars above,
    And sang to a small guitar,
"O lovely Pussy, O Pussy, my love,
    What a beautiful Pussy you are,
You are, you are!
    What a beautiful Pussy you are!"

Pussy said to the Owl, "You elegant fowl,
    How charmingly sweet you sing!
Oh! let us be married; too long we have tarried:
    But what shall we do for a ring?"

They sailed away, for a year and a day,
    To the land where the bong-tree grows;
And there in a wood a Piggy-wig stood,
    With a ring at the end of his nose,
His nose, his nose,
    With a ring at the end of his nose.

"Dear Pig, are you willing to sell for
    one shilling
    Your ring?" Said the Piggy, "I will."
So they took it away, and were married
    next day
    By the Turkey who lives on the hill.

They dined on mince and slices of quince,
    Which they ate with a runcible spoon;
And hand in hand, on the edge of the sand,
    They danced by the light of the moon,
The moon, the moon,
    They danced by the light of the moon.

EDWARD LEAR

Little Bo Peep has lost her sheep,
    And can't tell where to find them;
Leave them alone, and they'll come home,
    Bringing their tails behind them.

Little Bo Peep fell fast asleep,
    And dreamt she heard them bleating;
But when she awoke, she found it a joke,
    For they were still a-fleeting.

Then up she took her little crook,
    Determined for to find them;
She found them indeed,
    but it made her heart bleed
    For they'd left their tails behind them.

It happened one day, as Bo Peep did stray
    Into a meadow hard by,
There she espied their tails side by side,
    All hung on a tree to dry.

She heaved a sigh, and wiped her eye,
    And over the hillocks went rambling,
And tried what she could
    as a shepherdess should,
    To tack each again to its lambkin.

Little Miss Muffet
Sat on a tuffet,
Eating her curds and whey;
There came a big spider,
Who sat down beside her
And frightened Miss Muffet away.

Once a Mouse, a Frog, and a Little Red Hen,
    Together kept a house;
The Frog was the laziest of frogs,
    And lazier still was the Mouse.

The work all fell on the Little Red Hen,
    Who had to get the wood,
And build the fires, and scrub, and cook,
    And sometimes hunt the food.

One day, as she went scratching around,
    She found a bag of rye;
Said she, "Now who will make some bread?"
    Said the lazy Mouse, "Not I."

"Nor I," croaked the Frog
    as he drowsed in the shade,
    Red Hen made no reply,
But flew around with bowl and spoon,
    And mixed and stirred the rye.

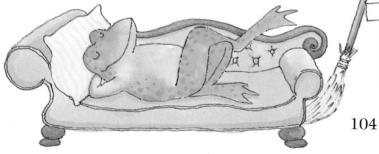

"Who'll make the fire to bake the bread?"
    Said the Mouse again, "Not I,"
And, scarcely opening his sleepy eyes,
    Frog made the same reply.

The Little Red Hen said never a word,
    But a roaring fire she made;
And while the bread was baking brown,
    "Who'll set the table?" she said.

"Not I," said the sleepy Frog with a yawn;
    "Nor I," said the Mouse again;
So the table she set and the bread put on,
    "Who'll eat this bread?" said the Hen.

"I will!" cried the Frog.
    "And I!" squeaked the Mouse
    As they near the table drew:
"Oh, no, you won't!" said the Little Red Hen,
    And away with the loaf she flew.

105

There was an old woman
    who lived in a shoe;
She had so many children
    she didn't know what to do.
She gave them some broth
    without any bread;
Then whipped them all soundly
    and put them to bed.

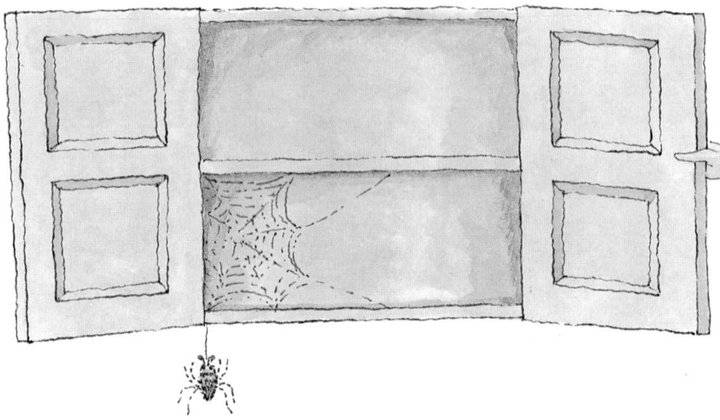

Old Mother Hubbard
    Went to her cupboard,
To fetch her poor dog a bone;
    But when she got there
    The cupboard was bare
And so the poor dog had none.

She went to the baker's
　　To buy him some bread;
But when she came back
　　The poor dog was dead.

She went to the tailor's
　　To buy him a coat;
But when she came back
　　He was riding a goat.

She went to the hatter's
　　To buy him a hat;
But when she came back
　　He was feeding the cat.

She went to the joiner's
　　To buy him a coffin;
But when she came back
　　The poor dog was laughing.

She went to the cobbler's
　　To buy him some shoes;
But when she came back
　　He was reading the news.

She went to the hosier's
　　To buy him some hose;
But when she came back
　　He was dressed in his clothes.

The dame made a curtsey,
　　The dog made a bow;
The dame said, "Your servant,"
　　The dog said, "Bow-wow."

Sicilian Lament

My pretty boy, what can I do?
Will you not give me one hour's relief?

LULLABIES

The Man in the Moon looked
    out of the moon,
Looked out of the moon
    and said:
"'Tis time for all children
    on the earth
To think about going to bed!"

Wee Willie Winkie runs through the town,
Upstairs and downstairs in his nightgown,
Rapping at the window, crying through the lock:
"Are all the children in their beds, it's past eight o'clock?"

Niddledy, noddeldy
To and fro.
Tired and sleepy,
To bed we go.

Jump into bed,
Switch out the light,
Head on the pillow,
Shut your eyes tight.

Lie abed,
Sleepy head,
Shut up eyes, Bo Peep;
Till daybreak
Never wake;
Baby sleep.

Twinkle, twinkle, little star,
How I wonder what you are!
Up above the world so high,
Like a diamond in the sky.

Then the traveler in the dark
Thanks you for your tiny spark;
He could not see which way to go,
If you did not twinkle so.

In the dark blue sky you keep
And often through my curtains peep,
For you never shut your eye
Till the sun is in the sky.

As your bright and tiny spark
Lights the traveler in the dark,
Though I know not what you are,
Twinkle, twinkle, little star.

Star light, star bright,
First star I see tonight,
I wish I may, I wish I might,
Have the wish I wish tonight.

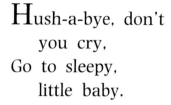

Hush-a-bye, don't
 you cry,
Go to sleepy,
 little baby.

When you wake, you
 shall have a cake
And all the pretty
 little horses.

Blacks and bays,
 dapples and grays,
Coach and six
 white horses.

Hush thee, my baby,
 Lie still with thy daddy,
Thy mammy has gone to the mill,
 To get some meal
 To bake a cake,
So pray, my dear baby, lie still.

Hush, little baby, don't say a word,
Papa's gonna buy you a mocking bird.

If that mocking bird won't sing,
Papa's gonna buy you a diamond ring.

If the diamond ring turns to brass,
Papa's gonna buy you a looking glass.

If that looking glass gets broke,
Papa's gonna buy you a billy goat.

If that billy goat won't pull,
Papa's gonna buy you a cart and a bull.

If that cart and bull turn over,
Papa's gonna buy you a dog named Rover.

If that dog named Rover won't bark,
Papa's gonna buy you a horse and cart,

If that horse and cart fall down,
You'll still be the sweetest baby in town.

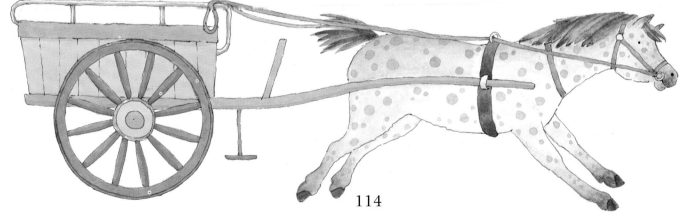

Sleepy time has come
   for my baby,
Baby now is going to sleep;
Kiss Mama goodnight and
   we'll turn out the light,
While I tuck you in beneath
   your covers tight;
Sleepy time has come
   for my baby,
Baby now is going to sleep.

Where should a baby rest?
Where but on its mother's arm
Where can a baby lie
Half so safe from every harm?
Lulla, lulla, lullaby,
Softly sleep, my baby
Lulla, lulla, lullaby,
Soft, soft, my baby.

Golden Slumbers

Golden slumbers kiss your eyes,
Smiles awake you when you rise.
   Sleep, pretty wantons, do not cry,
   And I will sing a lullaby:
Rock them, rock them, lullaby.

Care is heavy, therefore sleep you;
You are care and care must keep you.
   Sleep, pretty wantons, do not cry,
   And I will sing a lullaby:
Rock them, rock them, lullaby.

THOMAS DECKER

Hush-a-bye baby
On the tree top.
When the wind blows,
The cradle will rock;
When the bough breaks,
The cradle will fall;
Down will come baby,
Cradle and all.

Bye low, bye low,
Baby's in the cradle sleeping;
Tip toe, tip toe,
Still as pussy slyly creeping;
Bye low, bye low,
Rock the cradle, baby's waking;
Hush, my baby, oh!

Love Me

Love me—I love you,
    Love me, my baby;
Sing it high, sing it low,
    Sing it as may be.

Mother's arms under you,
    Her eyes above you
Sing it high, sing it low,
    Love me—I love you.

CHRISTINA ROSSETTI

Brahms' Lullaby

Lullaby and goodnight,
With lilies of white
And roses of red
To pillow your head:
May you wake when the day
Chases darkness away,
May you wake when the day
Chases darkness away.

Lullaby and goodnight,
Let angels of light
Spread wings round your bed
And guard you from dread.
Slumber gently and deep
In the dreamland of sleep,
Slumber gently and deep
In the dreamland of sleep.

JOHANNES BRAHMS

Sleep, baby, sleep.
Thy father guards the sheep;
Thy mother shakes the dreamland tree,
Down falls a little dream for thee:
Sleep, baby, sleep.

Sleep, baby, sleep.
The large stars are the sheep;
The little stars are the lambs, I guess,
And the gentle moon is the shepherdess;
Sleep, baby, sleep.

The White Seal's Lullaby

Oh! hush thee, my baby, the night is behind us,
    And black are the waters that sparkled so green.
The moon o'er the combers, looks downward to find us
    At rest in the hollows that rustle between.
Where billow meets billow, then soft be thy pillow;
    Ah, weary wee flipperling, curl at thy ease,
The storm shall not wake thee, nor shark overtake thee,
    Asleep in the arms of the slow-swinging seas.

RUDYARD KIPLING

A Child

What can lambkins do,
All the keen night through?
Nestle by their woolly mother,
The careful ewe.

What can nestlings do,
In the nightly dew?
Sleep beneath their mother's wing,
Till day breaks anew.

If in field or tree,
There might only be,
Such a warm, soft, sleep place,
Found for me!

CHRISTINA ROSSETTI

Sweet and Low

Sweet and low, sweet and low,
   Wind of the western sea.
Low, low, breathe and blow,
   Wind of the western sea!
   Over the rolling waters go,
   Come from the dying moon,
   and blow,
   Blow him again to me;
While my little one, while my
   pretty one, sleeps.

Sleep and rest, sleep and rest,
   Father will come to thee soon;
Rest, rest, on mother's breast,
   Father will come to thee soon;
   Father will come to his babe
   in the nest,
   Silver sails all out of the west
   Under the silver moon;
Sleep, my little one, my pretty
   one, sleep.

ALFRED, LORD TENNYSON

A Baby's Boat

Baby's boat's a silver moon
Sailing in the sky,
Sailing o'er a sea of sleep
While the stars float by.

Sail, baby, sail,
Out upon that sea;
Only don't forget to sail
Back again to me.

Baby's fishing for a dream,
Fishing far and near,
Her line a silver moonbeam is,
Her bait a silver star.

Sail, baby, sail
Out upon that sea;
Only don't forget to sail
Back again to me.

INDEX